Dedicated to brave babies,
just like Abel,
who spent many days, weeks,
and months in the NICU visited daily
by his twin brother Oren.

Although their journeys have all been different,
these tiny babies inspire us every day!

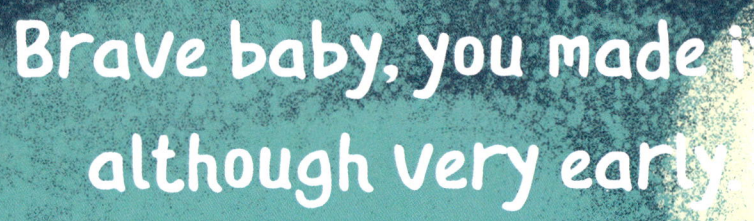

Brave baby, you made it
although very early

You catch a glimpse of your mama
as you're
whisked off in a hurry.

The bed seems quite warm,
but it's not the same.

You wish for your mama,
as you hear others say your name.

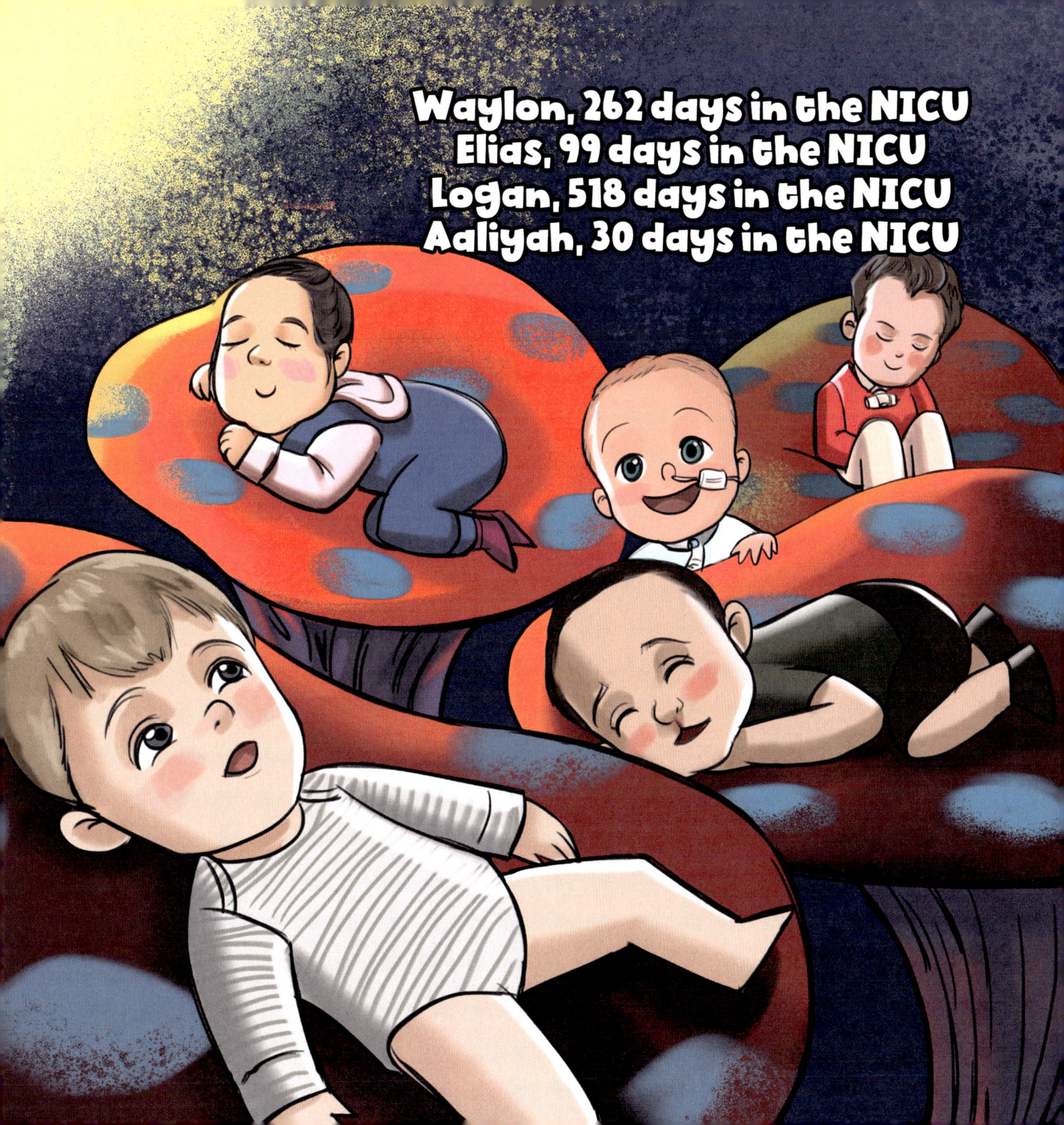

Everett, 44 days in the NICU
Evie, 54 days in the NICU
Aubree, 139 days in the NICU
Margaret, 150 days in the NICU

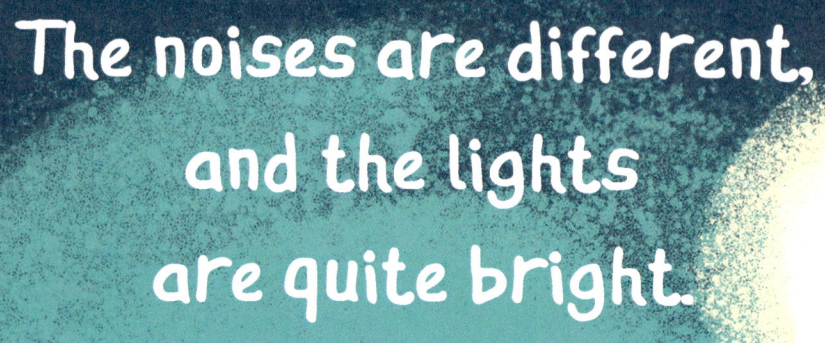

The noises are different,
and the lights
are quite bright.

You want to scream,
but you know that won't be polite.

You just wanted to meet her, your mommy, right now!

You waited as long as your patience would allow.

You know her immediately
and try to open your eyes.

She's more perfect than you imagined
and it's such a surprise!

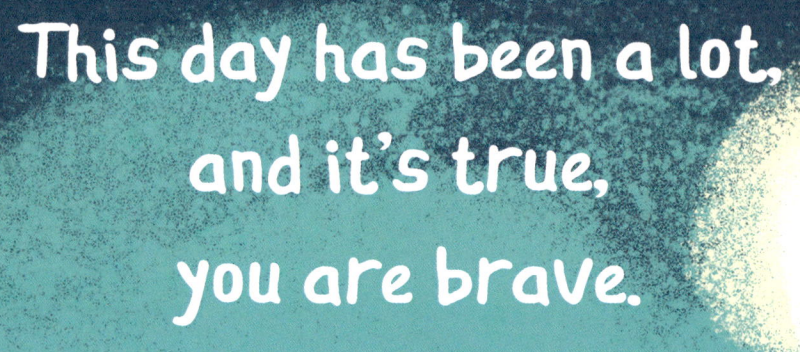

This day has been a lot,
and it's true,
you are brave.

But you knew it was her
and the love that she gave.

Each day when she comes is the best day ever.

She tells you that soon you'll be home together.

Someday soon, you'll be going home.
It's hard to wait.

But you'll be bigger and stronger, and there's no debate

When you are home,
you will never forget when...

You spent many days in the NICU,
and how brave you have been.

On August 26, 2023, Abel passed away suddenly.
He stabilized briefly to say goodbye to
his family, friends, and primary nurses.

He is greatly loved and missed beyond words.

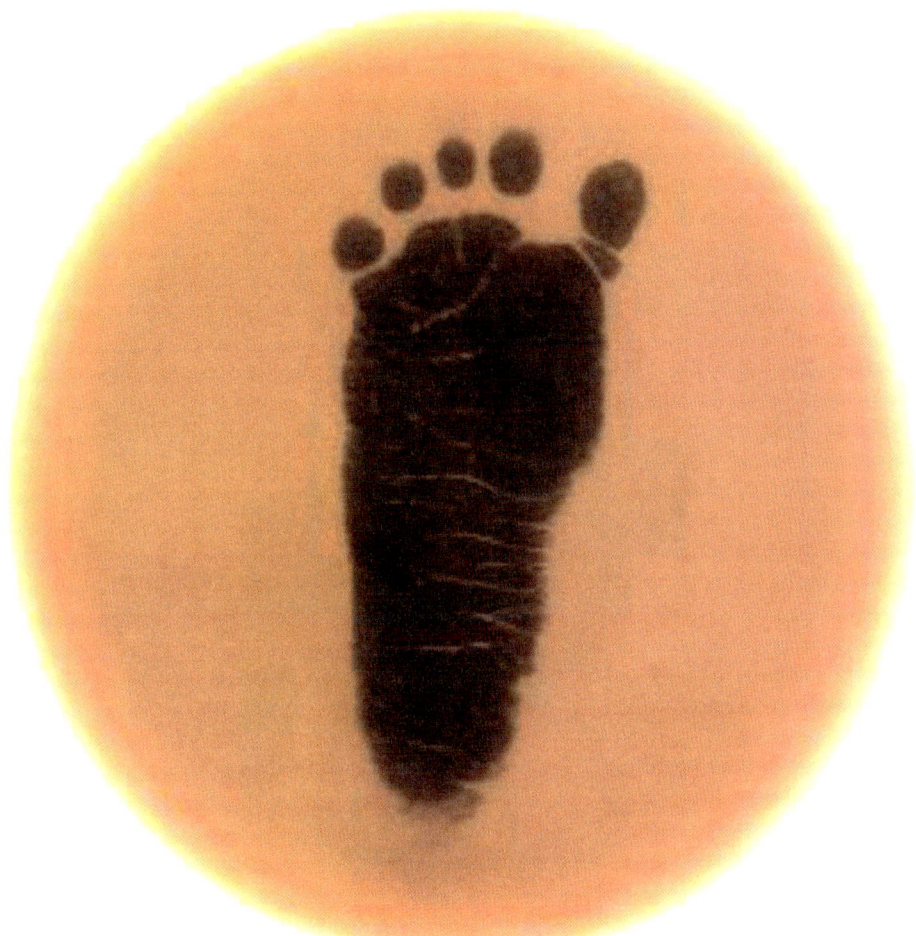

He will continue to live on through his books; inspiring hope, and
showing the worth and love of these amazing children no matter
the limitation or the duration of their beautiful lives.

Watch for the next books in the Born Abel Book Series:

The Great Baby Wait

What is a Mother,   Who's Who in the NICU

What is Heaven   and   The Extra Gift

   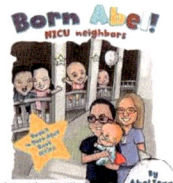  

Be sure to get your copies of Abel's first 10 books,
1st Workbook, 5 Coloring Books & 2 Journals:
All available on Amazon.com

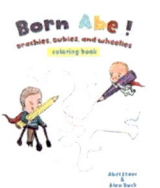       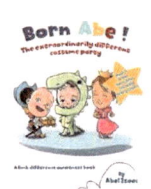

Remember:
All proceeds from the Born Abel Book Series go directly to the Born Abel Foundation!

Copyright © 2024 Born Abel Foundation

Published in the United States of America
All rights reserved worldwide

Authentic Endeavors Publishing / Book Endeavors
Clarks Summit PA 18411

Copyright © 2024 Illustrated by Emilian Rubio

No part of this book may be reproduced by any mechanical, photographic, or electronic process, or in the form of an audio or digital recording, nor may it be stored in any retrieval system, transmitted or otherwise, be copied for public or private use other than for fair use as brief quotation embodied in articles and review - without prior written permission of the author, illustrators or publisher.

Born Abel: Babies Born Brave

Paperback ISBN: 978-1-963849-09-7

Born Abel Book Series

Made in the USA
Las Vegas, NV
29 November 2024

12901772R00026